This book belongs to
the hairy pirate

NOAH ADAMS

loyal member of
Backbeard's crew.

# BACKBEARD

## AND THE BIRTHDAY SUIT

Walker & Company  New York

For Christy, and for Anthony, my favorite pirate —M. M.

First published in the United States of America in 2006 by Walker Publishing Company, Inc.
Paperback edition published in 2007
Distributed to the trade by Holtzbrinck Publishers

For information about permission to reproduce selections from this book, write to
Permissions, Walker & Company, 104 Fifth Avenue, New York, New York 10011

The Library of Congress has cataloged the hardcover edition as follows:
McElligott, Matthew.
Backbeard and the birthday suit / Matthew McElligott.
p.    cm.
Summary: Backbeard is a rough, tough, and very hairy pirate who decides to get a new suit for his birthday, only to find that pirate fashions are all out of style.
ISBN-13: 978-0-8027-8065-2  •  ISBN-10: 0-8027-8065-2 (hardcover)
ISBN-13: 978-0-8027-8066-9  •  ISBN-10: 0-8027-8066-0 (reinforced)
[1. Pirates–Fiction. 2. Clothing and dress–Fiction. 3. Cleanliness–Fiction.
4. Humorous stories–Fiction.]  I. Title.
PZ7.M478448Bab 2007          [E]–dc22          2007008065

ISBN-13: 978-0-8027-9680-6  •  ISBN-10: 0-8027-9680-X (paperback)

Book design by Nicole Gastonguay

The artist used pencil, fabric, photography, and digital techniques to create the illustrations for this book. All textures and colors throughout the book are photographs of real objects.

Visit Walker & Company's Web site at www.walkeryoungreaders.com

Printed in China
10 9 8 7 6 5 4 3 2 1

All papers used by Walker & Company are natural, recyclable products made from wood grown in well-managed forests. The manufacturing processes conform to the environmental regulations of the country of origin.

This is the story of Backbeard, the hairiest pirate ever.

Backbeard was so hairy, it was sometimes tough to tell if there was a pirate underneath.

Backbeard was also the toughest, loudest, most unsanitary pirate ever. This made it hard for him to keep a parrot. Most quit after the first few days.

Backbeard's ship, the *Five O'Clock Shadow*, was feared throughout the land.

On Backbeard's birthday, the entire crew put on their best clothes. They drank punch and scratched and spit. They hit each other with bottles and sang pirate songs. Then they had cake and opened presents. Afterward, Backbeard threw them all overboard.

"What a great party!" said Backbeard.

That night, alone in his cabin, Backbeard looked in the mirror.

His clothes were in tatters. His shirt was stained with punch. His pants had a hole the size of his bottom, and his underwear was full of frosting.

"Polly, I'm a mess," said Backbeard. "Even for a pirate."

"I quit," said the parrot.

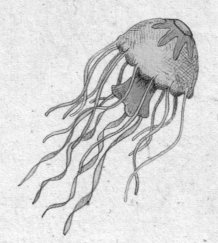

The next morning, Backbeard called the crew together.

"Listen up, you jellyfish," he bellowed. "I'm going into town for a while. Stay out of trouble or you'll walk the plank."

"You stink!" shouted one of the pirates.

"Don't come back!" called out another.

Someone threw an egg at Backbeard's hat.

"I love these guys!" thought Backbeard.

In town, Backbeard came to a small store. The window was filled with fancy clothes. Inside, a small, wiry man stood behind the counter.

"My, my!" said the man. "What are you supposed to be?"

"Shiver me timbers!" said Backbeard. "I'm a pirate!"

"Of course you are," said the man. "What happened to your pirate suit?"

"I had a birthday party," said Backbeard. "Is that a problem?"

"Not at all," said the man.

"First of all, I want a new hat," said Backbeard.

"What kind of hat?" asked the man.

"A pirate hat!" roared Backbeard.

"I'm afraid we don't have that," said the man.

"Blimey!" said Backbeard. "Then give me a bandana."

"How about a straw boater?"

"I don't know what that is," grumbled Backbeard.

"Trust me," said the man. "It's much nicer."

"Arrgh," sighed Backbeard.

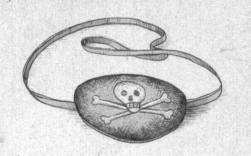

"I also need a new coat," said Backbeard. "Do you have anything in a buccaneer style?"

"I'm afraid not."

"Pirate pants?" asked Backbeard. "An eye patch?"

"I'd have to check."

"And I'll need a new parrot too," said Backbeard.

"I'm sorry," said the man. "We don't sell animals."

"Hogwash!" said Backbeard. "What's a pirate without a mascot?"

"Let me see what I can do," said the man.

When they were finished, the man said, "That will be seven pieces of eight, please."

"Blimey!" said Backbeard. "I don't pay for things—I'm a pirate! Besides, I look like a sissy."

"You do not," said the man. "You look very stylish."

"I do?" asked Backbeard.

"Certainly," said the man.

Backbeard looked in the mirror. He narrowed his eyes. He studied his reflection.

"I suppose I do at that!" thought Backbeard.

Outside, Backbeard noticed people staring at him.

"The poor landlubbers," thought Backbeard. "They're jealous of my suit."

He stopped a little girl on the street.

"Are you staring at me?"

"Yes, sir," said the girl. "You have pretty clothes."

"Thank you!" Backbeard laughed. "So do you!"

Back at the ship, the first mate, Sweaty McGhee, was standing watch.

"Halt, stranger!" shouted Sweaty. "Who goes there?"

"It's me, you stinkbottom!" Backbeard laughed. "Quit fooling around."

"Go away," said Sweaty. "If our captain catches you, you'll walk the plank."

"Drivelswigger!" roared Backbeard. "I am the captain!"

"Pffffffffffftttttt!" said Sweaty.

Backbeard wiped Sweaty's saliva from his eye. "Listen, you bottom-feeder, lower the gangplank or I'll have your hat. Shiver me timbers!"

"You *sound* like the captain," said Sweaty, "but you *look* like a goofball."

"What's all the hubbub?" said Mad Garlic Jack.

"Garlic, this lubber calls himself the cap'n. What say we go down there and batten his hatch?"

"I'm with ye, Sweaty," said Mad Garlic Jack. "Gather the mates and let's have at him!"

"Do your worst, you barnacled scallywags!" roared Backbeard.

"But wrinkle my suit and you'll swab the deck for a year!"

But the fight didn't cheer Backbeard up at all. "Pig," he said, "I'm starting to think these clothes were a bad idea."

"Hwuuuungk!" snorted the pig.

Backbeard turned to the crew. "Listen, guys," he said, "can we be serious for a moment?"

The pirates nodded. They were in no mood to argue.

"This new outfit, does it work for me?"

"It's certainly different," said Mad Garlic Jack. "Maybe we just need time to get used to it."

"Do you like it, Cap'n?" asked Sweaty McGhee.

"I do," said Backbeard.

"Well then, that's all that counts, ain't it?" said Sweaty.

"I'm thinking of the other pirates," said Backbeard. "Will they still respect me?"

"Hornswoggle," said Mad Garlic Jack. "You're still the hairiest pirate to sail the five seas. A fancy suit and a pig don't change that."

"And you're still stupid," offered Scarlet Doubloon.

"And you still stink!" said Sweaty McGhee.

Backbeard looked at his crew. He adjusted his coat. He brushed off his sleeves. Someone threw an egg at his hat.

"I love you guys," said Backbeard.